PASSAGES

PASSAGES

A LONG DAY'S JOURNEY INTO LIFE

D. Allen Butcher

WHERE DID THEY GO?

"So-and-So just passed away."

I hear that from day to day.

But when did that passage begin?

I know about the end.

And where is the "away" that

they went away to on that day?

The answer to the first

goes back to the day of birth.

The second will be decided

by the Creator of the earth.

An Original Poem By
D. Allen Butcher

To Margaret

who encouraged me.

PREFACE

The idea for *Passages* came about in an unusual way. I was dining with my favorite retired English professor when the conversation turned to the journey we are all on in this life. The words of an old Gospel song suddenly popped into my mind, which I proceeded to emote as follows:

This World Is Not My Home.

I'm Just A-Passing Through.

My Treasures Are Laid Up,

Somewhere Beyond The Blue.

Old Time Gospel Song by J.R. Baxter

As I belabored those lyrics, the words "passing through" stuck in my mind. What would it be like to trace one man's journey through a circle of life on a time-train, beginning at birth, previewing each stop along the way with the dangers and challenges that had to be faced for his journey to continue until its end, when he would return to the Creator and the stream of eternity? And so, the project was launched.

To try to put a label on this work is difficult. I would tend to call it an adult development narrative with spiritual and autobiographical overtones. That's a mouthful, but it's all that I could come up with. It is what it is. While this is written as a man's passage, there is something here for women as well. As a woman, you might discover similar challenges in your own passage. Plus, it might help you to understand the significant male in your life at various stages of his life. Apparently, no one has attempted to write about a woman's passage, as no one has ever been able to fully understand women- only kidding, of course. Are men that simple? This book should appeal to anyone interested in the cycle of life. Some might say it was a book that had to be written.

So, as they say in the travel industry: "Sit back, relax, and enjoy the trip!" You might find yourself at a stop along the way.

D. Allen Butcher

TABLE OF CONTENTS

PRE-DEPARTURE

"We are all visitors to this time, this place. We are just passing through. Our purpose here is to observe, to learn, to grow, to love, and then we return home."

Queen Elizabeth II

Greetings! Let me introduce myself. I am a representative of Father Time (some erroneously call me a Guardian Angel), and I have been assigned to give you a preview of a passage we call life on planet Earth.

As Adam sinned in the beginning, the Creator was obligated to render punishment. Accordingly, man was condemned to live a life in time, in the weakness of human flesh, with the possibility of redemption at the end.

You have been selected to leave the stream of eternity and enter this loop of time. Your assignment is to accomplish your purpose in life. Finding that assignment will come at some point in your passage. You are already known by God, so don't try to blend in and lose your identity. In the season of your manifestation, take my advice early on: Seek the Lord's perfect will. Commit your life to the one who brought you here and depend on Him to guide you.

When your passage is complete, you will return to the stream of eternity. There, you will receive an evaluation and placement based on your performance. I have been on many of these passages, so it would do you well to listen up to this preview as we go along. Your destiny is determined by your beginning, so let's begin.

Let me pull your folder and see what the setting is for your passage. Ah, yes, here it is. Just scanning it, I can already see that you will begin with many advantages compared to others. You are to embark in the first half of the twenty-first century in the United States of America— a time of great division and violence, as I recall. But take heart, I'm here to guide you and to give you a preview of the challenges you will face at each stop on your passage. Try not to nod off. This is important stuff.

Let's see what else is in your dispatch folder. I see that your sex has been assigned as "Male." There seems to be a lot of confusion on this issue about where you are going. Male and Female are the only ones assigned, but some are confused about which one they are. Some want to change from one to the other and use different pronouns. That creates its own problem. Just stay with your assignment, and your passage will be much smoother.

I also see that the Creator has predestinated you to be one of His. That means that a supernatural call will be placed in your soul at birth. You will respond to that call at some point in your passage.

Well, that just about completes my pre-departure briefing. Whatever I have missed will be covered down-line. It's time now to go to the embarkation point—your mother's womb.

CHAPTER 1
GENESIS

Before you were formed in the womb...I knew you.

Jerimiah 1:5

I forgot to mention that you were also predestined to make your appearance on the earth at this specific time, ordained by your Creator. Your forebears are right now meeting and contributing their individual cornucopia of DNA in a process called "conception." (Can we give them a little privacy?)

This begins the process of knitting and forming you in the relative safety of your mother's womb. I say 'relative' because the womb can be a dangerous place, depending on your mother. I've heard that any woman has the potential to produce a baby, but not every woman is a real mother. And so, the dangers of your passage begin here.

That first danger begins as you are being formed. Each process has an "inspector" on a formation assembly line, assigning various attributes and characteristics based on DNA, and checking for defects.

Removal from the assembly line is called a "miscarriage", a passage that is terminated before it can begin. At times, defects get by the inspector and become a permanent part of the finished product, transported with a label reading "handicapped," a label that will produce a remarkably different passage.

I believe I recall a poem that speaks to those who are born as such. Excuse me a moment while I look in my files. Ah, yes, here it is! It was written by the poet Marion Peck and entitled "Gifts," and it reads as follows:

I saw a child who could not see.

Dear Lord, I cried, why should this be?

Never to look on the face of love...

Or the sun...or the trees...or the stars above.

Always to walk through eternal night...

Never to know the comfort of life?

I saw a child, no steps, who could take.

Dear Lord, I cried, my heart doth ache!

Never to stand up straight or tall...

This child, though he tries, can only fall...

What did he do to be made this way?

'Tis every child's right to run and play!

I saw a child who could speak no word.

Isn't this cruel, I cried, Dear Lord?

And he cannot hear, on top of it all...

Never can hear his mother call...

Never to speak...never to hear...

I turned my face to hide a tear.

I saw a child who could not reason.

Locked away for his whole life's season...

Locked away and all unaware

Of the world of the mind, the others share.

Dear Lord, I said, why this affliction?

Denying this child of the mind's benediction?

Then spoke a voice through my heart to me:

"THESE ARE THE GIFTS I GIVE TO THEE"

That little child will take your hand

And lead you through this weary land...

And show you wonders beyond compare...

And beauty you never dreamed was there.

And that little boy so crippled and lame

Has courage, My Son, that would put yours to shame.

He'll teach you to walk if you'll just hold his hand...

To walk upright with your fellow man.

And the little girl there whose tongue could not speak...

Can teach you the eloquence of tears on a cheek.

You'll learn that the heart can volumes tell

If it's warmed by love and care as well.

And that mindless one...Hold the cup to his lips

And you'll find that God's love you also will sip.

Perhaps your mind's closed, but you hold the key

And when you open to him, you open to Me

Dear Lord, I said, I humbly thank Thee.

I'll live for these children...who are Your Gifts to me.

Glad I had a Kleenex for that one. As you can see, God has a special mission for each passage, handicap or no. But I digress. Let's get back to your embarkation location and look at more of those dangers.

The next danger to a successful beginning is the attitude of the mother. Does she want you? Or are you a mistake that happened at an inconvenient time? Will she carry you or have your passage terminated by a process called abortion"? Some say that those whose passages have been terminated in this manner go immediately back into the presence of the Creator. That could be a good or a bad thing, depending on how the passage might have gone.

Or, perhaps she will birth you and place you in a dumpster, try to flush you down a toilet, or, at best, leave you on a doorstep or in a "Baby Box" located at the nearest fire station. Your assigned mother can be your worst enemy early on. But, not to worry. Your dispatch folder indicates that you have been assigned a loving mother who wants you. Unfortunately, you don't come with an owner's manual, so give her a little slack.

I will now fast-forward your timeline by approximately nine months—not that those months are not important. You are being prepped for your entrance into the world. Think of it as being in an oven until you are "done".

Assuming that you survive the dangers of the womb, you will miraculously emerge into the light of day without any complication- a living example of the highest form of creation.

One of America's founding documents says that "all men are created equal." And that is true within the context of conception. What it doesn't say is that "all men are born into equal circumstances," which is a different animal altogether. Let's look at your circumstances.

While some of my clients were born in a dirt-floored hut somewhere in Africa, you are fortunate to have been born at the other end of the spectrum, a sterile delivery room in an upscale hospital. It makes a sizable difference, and you don't get to choose. In fact, you will have no choice about anything for some time to come. It appears, by the way, that you will be born into a typical American family. Let me pause here for a moment and review what occurs at your moment of birth.

As the Creator breathes into you that first breath of life and you become a living soul, your name is inscribed in the Book of Life with a date and a dash. Your passage has begun. What's the meaning of the dash, you might ask? It represents your allotted time before the end of your earthly passage, at which time an ending date will be inscribed. As your body returns to the dust of the earth, your spirit breaks up, and your soul returns to that stream of eternity I mentioned earlier.

What time factor can you expect when you consider the dash? The Creator's Holy Bible says, "three score and ten years, eighty if you have the strength." There is no mention of time beyond. One of my previous clients used a sports analogy. He called it "overtime"- remembering that those contests normally end with the team that scores first. It's called "sudden death."

Having seen many human newborns, I'm reminded of the sea turtle that scrambles across the sand at birth, seeking the safety of the ocean before sea birds can take their toll. I'm also reminded of the Wildebeest herds on the Serengeti Plains of Africa. After the female gives birth, the calf is on its feet and ready to run with its mother within hours.

But you will be less than a sea turtle or a Wildebeest- lying helpless in your mother's blood with no means of locomotion and totally dependent on what is to come. Plus, you will need years to fully develop. Is this some cruel joke instituted by the Creator, or is there a purpose here that we have yet to understand?

A sharp smack on your backside will bring you into a state of consciousness, and you will let out a cry, signaling your arrival to expectant ears. Strange that you will enter the world crying. But considering what man has wrought on this earth, there is every reason to do so. I have seen many tears in my passages- more for some, less for others. Circumstances and the choices you make down the line will be the determining factor.

After the cord is cut, tying you to your mother, you will now be on your own, ready (with considerable assistance) to navigate the obstacle course called "life". Your worldly passage has now begun.

CHAPTER 2
INFANCY

"All We Are Is Dust In The Wind"

Song By Kansas

As you begin your passage in the hospital, the usual protocol is to get you cleaned up, wrapped in the appropriate colored blanket (blue for you, pink for that other human species called female), and placed in a bassinet near a large window. Here, family and friends will come to ooh and ahh over you and try to figure out which family relative you favor.

By this time, you will have been given a name--one that will serve as an ID on your passage--one that you may or may not like. You can blame your parents later. You will also receive a birth certificate at this time, verifying that you are who you are, and given a date of embarkation. Think of it as a "ticket to ride."

But wait! More danger! You will now have to navigate the minefield of "first-year infant mortality." Considering that you will be one of a thousand, twenty-nine of you will have your passage cut short during this period.

The causes are too numerous to list, but range from malnutrition to infectious diseases to crib death. If you are fortunate, your mother will have refrained from drug use and alcohol consumption during her pregnancy, giving you a head start on your journey.

Immunizations, if available, will keep you safe from diphtheria, tetanus, polio, and whooping cough. With your shot record up-to-date, you will now be ready to go home, hopefully with those loving parents who have prepared a place for you.

Your home arrival will be cause for a family celebration. But wait! Another personage, somewhat older, has apparently beaten you to the home environment. He or she is called "sibling" and will be your competition for many things, and perhaps for many years.

Studies of the nesting pattern of the American Bald Eagle have shown that the eaglet that hatches first will attempt to kill its younger and weaker siblings in competition for food. You are not an eaglet, but there is potential danger here. Have you heard the biblical story of two brothers named Cain and Abel? You can look it up in the Holy Bible later.

There is one advantage to growing up with siblings, however. Learning to share will come to you soon enough.

Plus, you will naturally have better survival skills because you will already be trained in physical combat, psychological warfare, and sensing suspicious activity.

Your goal now will be to grow and thrive, avoiding the specter of infant mortality and other dangers associated with your environment.

If you are fortunate, your best source of food will be the milk at your mother's breast, although there are substitutes that will suffice without the nourishment quotient of the former (Goat's milk is made for baby goats). Ready for an interesting fact? Baby whales are known to gain 198 pounds per day on the rich milk from their mother. You will not be a baby whale, but, statistically, in 5 months, you should double your birth weight. Breast or bottle? Go for it!

I once had a passage with an airline pilot who could attest to the rule that no flight could leave the departure gate without at least one crying baby on board. Or at least it seemed that way to him. Crying is what you do at this stage of your passage because you have no other means of communicating your needs. Hungry? Cry! Dirty diaper? Cry! You get the picture. For your caregiver(s), this sends out an alarm, requiring eventual, if not immediate attention.

One of my clients, who had her first child, called this period "overwhelming"- one full year of sleepless nights catering to you, the little dictator. You might consider "sleeping through the night," a condition much appreciated by your relieved caretakers.

We now need to look at some other dangers that will be lurking in this phase of your passage. God forbid, but if your mother should become single again, you might become subject to the "abusive boyfriend syndrome". Statistics show that you will be forty times more likely to be abused, injured, or killed by a new man on the scene than if your birth parents are happily joined together.

Looking for a prime example in nature? Consider the young African lion who takes over the pride from an old outgoing male. His first action is to kill all the cubs sired by that male, thus eliminating that bloodline and starting his own. The worst part of this scenario is that the mother lionesses don't put up much of a fight. Hopefully, a divorced mother in this situation will choose her male companionship very carefully.

Another danger lurking along this stage of your passage is "hot car death". More than 900 infant passages have been cut short since 1990 after being left in a car where the temperature can rise to more than 170 degrees. While legislation is ongoing to place child alarms in new vehicles, the deaths continue to grow. Leaving an underage child alone in a vehicle under any circumstances is increasingly considered a crime. Hopefully, your caregivers are educated on this point.

Let's assume that you have avoided all the snares and dangers in your passage thus far and have reached the end of your first year. No time to celebrate, although your caregivers will most likely produce a birthday cake with one lighted candle, put a celebratory hat on your head, let you dig into the cake with your bare hands, and take dozens of photos and/or videos to show to others who may or may not be interested. Don't all babies look alike?

DANGER AHEAD!

You are about to enter the

"TODDLER ZONE"

CHAPTER 3
THE TODDLER

The grass withers and the flowers fall,
But the Word of our God endures forever.

Isaiah 40:8

Your passage will have now brought you into a new phase of growth and development: the toddler stage, defined as ages 1-3. Herein, you will have a rapid increase in energy, motor skills, and curiosity about the world around you. You will discover your voice and, among gurgling sounds, begin to develop your vocabulary. Mom and dad might compete, hoping you will first say "ma-ma" or "da-da."

Early on, you will be a "rug rat," just learning to sit without assistance, rocking back and forth on all fours, and starting to crawl. Hooray! You will have reached parity with the baby sea turtle.

One day, you might decide to pull up on a piece of furniture. Bingo! You will now be *homo erectus*, standing on your own two feet. Then comes that glorious day when, coaxed by mother or dad, you will turn loose of the furniture and take that unsupported first step.

Chinese philosopher Lao Tzu once said that "a long journey begins with a single step." You will have now taken that step. How many steps will your passage entail? Only time will tell.

You will now begin to develop some independence, the beginning of having a mind of your own. The period of crying for what you want will be largely over, although you might resort to that if you think it might sway your caregivers. This behavior is called a "tantrum" and can have any number of consequences- both good and bad.

This period of your passage is called the "terrible twos" and is designed to test your parents' patience. If they are smart, they will call for a "timeout," extract you from the situation, and try to convince you that such behavior is unacceptable. Spanking your bottom has also been known to work for past generations of parents.

Unfortunately, this part of your passage is also fraught with a variety of dangers as you will begin to explore the world around you. These include injuries such as falls, burns, drowning, fires, and medication poisoning, among others.

Another danger is being involved in a car crash. Your caregivers, in this timeframe, were required, by law, to place you in an approved car seat, rear-facing at first and then forward-facing to protect your neck and spine as you grow. In ancient times, there were no car seats, seat belts, or airbags in cars. A mother's arm was about all you could depend on. You, however, will be one of the fortunate ones. Welcome to the world of modern automotive engineering safety.

Protection from animals is important as well, particularly certain breeds of dogs that can kill. The Pit Bull, for example, has killed 272 children since 1980. Being short in stature and unable to defend yourself against such a threat can terminate your passage before its time.

This is not to say that having a dog in your household is bad. In fact, just the opposite is true. Research has shown that children who grow up around dogs have an improved immune system and are 30 percent less likely to experience colds, ear infections, and coughs than those who are not so exposed. In addition, you are given a life lesson in responsibility, lead a more active lifestyle, and learn about unconditional love—just to name a few of the benefits. Parents who understand all this will present you with a "fur-baby" early on. I always thought that the "Goldendoodle" was a good choice.

Hopefully, your caregivers will have "baby-proofed" the house by now, putting potential danger out of your reach. One final danger that needs special attention for your caregivers is the safe storage of guns. In the year 2021, guns accounted for 4,572 lives lost among children under the age of eighteen. And, the number is increasing.

Did I hear you say that you wanted to go back into the womb? Take courage, young traveler. There is much more to come. You are now about to make the next stop on your passage.

CHAPTER 4
EARLY CHILDHOOD

We Are Here For Only A Moment

Visitors And Strangers In The Land.

As Our Ancestors Were Before Us

Our Days On Earth Are Like A Passing

Shadow, Gone So Soon Without A Trace.

Chronicles 29:15

Your stop at this station will require a "layover' of approximately three years- ages 4 through 6. One day, a large yellow vehicle, labeled "school bus," will stop on the street near your home. It will be your first day of school. After you pose for a photo in your new school clothes, you will board the bus. From this point on, your life and your caregivers' lives will never be quite the same. You will have been launched into the world of education, where you will begin a period of development in many areas. The knot that tied you to the home environment has now been loosened. Your innocent, imaginative, and unprejudiced mind will now be assailed by the forces of good and evil. As the tree is bent, so will it grow.

You will now begin to develop the language skills needed to communicate with those around you. First, let's settle down with a good book. If you are fortunate, you will have been "read to" from the massive collection of children's books. This will give you a tremendous head start in becoming a man of letters. Learning to read is a critical step in your passage. Learning to retain and communicate what you read is a step forward in forming your intellect.

As you enter that first classroom, you will notice that there are others beginning their passage with you. These make up what is known as your "peer group". These fellow passengers can have a positive influence on your development. They can also have a negative influence, which we will cover in a future passage stopover.

You may also notice that a number of your fellow classmates have a different skin color. This age-old factor has created a prejudiced view by some who believe that one color is superior to another. This view is called "racism," which has manifested itself in a variety of ways, including ethnic conflicts, genocide, slavery, lynchings, segregation, Native American reservations, boarding schools, racist immigration and naturalization laws, and internment camps.

While racial discrimination has been banned and determined to be socially and morally unacceptable during the time of your passage, it remains a major phenomenon reflected in socioeconomic inequality. Fortunately, it does not come into play to any extent for you at this stop. However, it might rear its head downline. One of my previous clients recounted a child's song that always reminded him that the term "racist" is not applicable to the Creator. I am not a singer, but I think it went something like this:

"Jesus loves the little children
All the children of the world.
Red and yellow, black and white,
They are precious in His sight.
Jesus loves the little children of the world."

Young, old, or whatever color, God loves all His children. Adopt this attitude and you will have no trouble downline.

Seeing members of your peer group excel in academics can motivate you to higher performance--sort of an early form of "keeping up with the Joneses". Competition with others will become a mainstay in your passage.

At this point, you will begin to develop social skills as well: things like empathy and respect for others, learning to settle disputes and conflicts in a peaceful manner, and learning to cooperate and play well with others. There are many opportunities to experiment with new roles and interactions during this phase as well.

Hopefully, you will have good teachers and counselors, along with family members, who will guide and encourage you during this period. Perhaps you will begin your spiritual journey here as well- hearing the stories from the Holy B-I-B-L-E (Basic Instruction Before Leaving Earth) and knowing that you have a Creator who loves you and wants to bless you. Following His teachings will allow you to obtain all of His redemptive blessings.

Did I mention that your destiny is not your own? Your Creator has a plan for your life as you are one of His. But He has given you "free moral agency". That's the right to choose and make your own decisions during your passage. How you exercise that right relative to His plan will largely determine the quality of your journey.

In addition to the dangers previously mentioned in your stop at the Toddler station, there are two others to be aware of as you continue to this next stop in your passage.

The first of these is death by drowning. According to statistics, over 35,000 people experience death by drowning each year in the United States, 7,000 of them under the age of 14. And the number is increasing. It is critical that you learn to swim at this stage and to exercise caution around any body of water. Access to swimming lessons and other water safety skills training can save your life. Again, hopefully your parents will follow up on this point.

The second danger to consider is death or injury by fire. According to statistics, approximately 488 children under age 14 die in US home fires each year, and 16,600 are injured by fire/burn incidents. Playing with matches or around any open flame can lead to spreading fire and possible death or injury. Touching hot objects can also lead to serious burns and scarring.

As an aside, I always recall the words of Smokey the Bear: "Only <u>you</u> can prevent forest fires," <u>and</u> injury to yourself (my addition)

If you have avoided all the passage-ending dangers up to this point, you will now be ready to continue to the next station. Be of good courage. You are about to enter.

The Pre-Teen Zone

CHAPTER 5
PRE-TEEN (TWEEN)

"Ain't it Funny How Time Slips Away"

Song by Willie Nelson

This stopover will encompass your passage from approximately 6 to 12 years of age. I call it the "awkward" age as you try to establish an identity. One of my clients said it this way:

"At that age, I was too old to ride my bicycle and too young to drive a car past my girlfriend's house".

Discovering who you are will be a daunting task as the forces of your environment begin to shape your personality. Don't let the world tell you who you are. That is for you to decide.

Here comes that peer group again! You will look around and see things about others that you admire and want to emulate. Conversely, you will see things in others that you don't particularly like and will dismiss as something you don't care to add to your identity.

If your parents have been vigilant in your upbringing, you will have now begun to understand the difference between right and wrong. We call this developing a moral code—a code that will guide you in the choices you make during your passage. I remember one of my clients who had developed a good moral code but had a tendency to depart from it on occasion. Here is his story as he told it to me.

How I Set the World Record

In the 50 Meter Hurdles

It's said that you should be careful about delving into the sins of your past. But it is also said that confession is good for the soul. Accordingly, I have a confession to make. As a young boy, I had an addictive taste for watermelon-- other people's watermelons. Nothing tastes better than the heart of a freshly purloined melon straight from the field, broken open and consumed by moonlight. Almost every boy in our community knew who was growing melons that year, so it was just a matter of waiting for the right time to plan a raid.

We had been keeping an eye on one neighbor's field, so one moonlit night in August, we eased down the road, crossed a barbed wire fence, and found ourselves in watermelon heaven. I was in the process of removing the "mother of all melons" from her stem when I heard the unmistakable sound of the slide on a pump shotgun loading a shell into the chamber of the barrel.

As I turned toward the noise, I saw a tall, dark figure step out of the adjacent cornfield holding the shotgun mentioned above. It was at that moment that I began my record run, fully expecting to feel the sting of buckshot on my backside as I cleared the fence, ripping the seat out of my blue jeans.

It was right then that I decided to forever give up my life of crime, trusting that my sin had been cast into God's Sea of Forgetfulness, as though it never happened in the first place.

Today, watermelons are available year-round in every supermarket, if you want to call the seedless, almost-tasteless variety offered a real watermelon. Too, very few farmers bother with planting the real thing anymore, and young men are kept busy participating in organized activities and playing video games. I suppose that is a good thing, but if one of them knows the location...... No wait! Forget I said that.

That story always gives me a good laugh, but I think you get the idea. Developing a moral code is important. Sticking to it is the key.

As we continue in this phase of your passage, you will want to acquire some basic physical skills, like learning to tie your shoes and dressing yourself. At some point, you will be introduced to the "3 R's"—Reading, Riting, and Rithmitic. (I never thought those last two were spelled corrcctly) The most important of these is learning to read.

As I mentioned previously, having been "read to" as a toddler will give you a tremendous head start. Hopefully, you will have teachers who will encourage you and introduce you to the world of literature based on your reading level.

Closely associated with learning to read is learning to write. Unfortunately, the point at which your timeline enters this period, writing skills are on a steep decline. The days of teaching and learning the beautiful cursive writing styles of the past have been virtually abandoned. Rather than drawing your alphabet letters on paper, you will learn to type them on a computer keyboard or, on what is called an iPhone, used for sending messages. Newer is not always better in my opinion.

While you are learning to read and write, we can't leave out the importance of learning about numbers as well. Knowing how to add, subtract, multiply, and divide is a basic skill that will aid you in many situations during your passage. Committing them to memory will require repetition and practice.

By this point in your passage, you will have developed a state of stability. You are learning to focus and concentrate—a key to studying and making good grades in school. You are developing self-control and adapting it appropriately in various situations.

I had a previous client who received his first report card in the third grade with the following remark included by his teacher:

"Allen is a very bright student. However, he disturbs quite a bit."

Learning self-control and what is acceptable behavior in various situations is important as you move forward.

As your body begins a period of rapid growth, you will probably experience "growing pains"—periods of aching and throbbing in your legs and other extremities. Your skeletal bones are growing, and your "baby fat" is being replaced by muscle tissue. You look taller and thinner. You are gaining over 2 inches in height and 6.5 pounds in weight on average each year. The genetics passed down to you from your parents will play an important part in this process. As you approach the end of this stopover, you might also notice the appearance of small amounts of hair on various parts of your body, accompanied by acne and body odor. You will have come a long way, baby. Hang in there.

Also important at this station is developing the ability to find and keep friends. I once heard a wise man say that to have a friend, you must first be friendly. That idea seems to have worked for all my clients. Making friends and keeping friends are important in so many ways.

Friendships help develop your self-esteem and confidence. This will give you a sense of belonging and identity. Participating in activities with your age group will help you learn to share and to resolve conflicts. Hopefully, your parents will encourage these activities and guide you away from the distractions of video games, social media, and television.

It is very important that you choose your friends carefully. A good friend will always have your best interest at heart, versus one who will not. Also, your reputation will be known by the company you keep. Wise men have said: "Show me your friends and I will show you who you are," and "If you sleep with dogs that have fleas, you will get fleas." I think you will get the idea when you enter this phase of your passage.

As a great part of your interaction with other children will take place in the school environment, you could be subjected to what is called "bullying." This is abuse, either physical or mental, by another person who is bigger and stronger than you. In your passage time frame, schools are working with teachers and parents to help solve this problem and to make the learning environment safe for everyone. In earlier times, this problem was solved by giving the bully a punch in the nose. Not that I recommend that, as it could escalate to a higher level of conflict.

Let me stop right here and issue a warning about another danger in this phase of your passage. Because there are bad people out there who want to molest or kidnap you, it is very important that you remember this rule: If someone you don't know offers you a ride or a candy treat, use the NO-GO-YELL-TELL formula. Firmly say "NO" and "GO" (run away to find a safe place). YELL to attract the attention of anyone close by who could help with your rescue. Finally, TELL-talk about your encounter to your parents, or someone in authority, who will take it from there.

In the United States, a child is abducted every 40 seconds for various reasons. Some never return. Don't become a statistic. Stay under the protection of your caregivers and other responsible adults.

Now, where were we? Oh yes, here we are

After you are well-established in your schoolwork, you will want to consider some extra-curricular activities.

The first of these is sports. In your timeframe, only 24% of this age group are getting the daily recommendation of 60 minutes of exercise. It's important that your parents find ways for you to be more physically active. Participation in sports has many health benefits. In addition, it builds self-esteem and helps build additional social skills.

The important thing is to find a sports activity that fits you and that you enjoy- one that could even continue over the entirety of your passage. One of my clients chose running track at this age and became a champion in that sport. I would bet that he is still running somewhere downline. But there are many other sports that will be available to you at your school or in your community.

Several of my past clients chose baseball. And, after starting off playing "catch" with Dad in the back yard, went on to excel at the highest levels of the sport. I particularly remember one client and his son who chose football at this age. They both went on to play at the collegiate and professional levels.

There are many other sports, both team and individual, you might consider. These include all the "ball" sports: soccer, volleyball, basketball, golf, tennis, etc. Other sports include wrestling, swimming, gymnastics, and archery. The list goes on and on. Whichever of these you choose, start slowly, learn the rules, and follow the teaching of your coaches and mentors.

I had previously mentioned the dangers of guns back at the Toddler station, but there are sports that involve guns that can be enjoyed by young people under the close supervision of an adult. Shooting sports such as skeet and trap are enjoyed by many people throughout their passages. Passing a gun safety course is paramount before handling a firearm.

If your father is an outdoor sportsman, he will most likely introduce you to hunting and fishing. I once had a client who loved to deer hunt. One time, he related a story about one of his hunts that demonstrated that love. Here is the way he told it to me:

THE DEER HUNT

It was pitch black as I settled into my deer stand. Dead silence in the woods. No creature stirring. A time to meditate on the good things of life and to thank the good Lord for his bountiful blessings. As the twilight came on, I could begin to distinguish the trees and underbrush around me. And then it began- the faint chirp of a bird, the rustle of a chipmunk in the leaves, the sound of a squirrel as it scurried down a nearby hickory tree, the first cawing of a distant flock of crows, the lowing of a cow in the distance, the crow of a rooster. The sky in the east was now illuminated with the coming dawn. As the sun peeked over the ridge, the forest was filled with shafts of sunlight. Suddenly, a doe and her fawn appeared in the clearing near my stand, pawing for acorns. There would be no killing in the woods this morning- nothing of man to interrupt the magic of another day.

Well, that was uplifting. I had another client who loved to fish. He was a real sportsman who always released his catch. He pointed me to a poem by Elizabeth Bishop that influenced him to adopt that habit. It went something like this:

THE FISH

*I caught a tremendous fish and held him beside the boat half out
of water, with my hook fast in a corner of his mouth. He didn't
fight. He hadn't fought at all. He hung a grunting weight,
battered and venerable and homely. Here and there, his brown
skin hung in strips like ancient wallpaper, and its pattern of
darker brown was like wallpaper: shapes like full-blown roses
stained and lost through age. He was speckled with barnacles,
fine rosettes of lime, and infested with tiny white sea-lice, and
underneath two or Three rags of green weed hung down. While
his gills were breathing in the terrible oxygen —the frightening
gills, fresh and crisp with blood, that can cut so badly— I
thought of the coarse white flesh packed in like feathers, the big
bones and the little bones, the dramatic reds and blacks of his
shiny entrails, and the pink swim bladder, like a big peony. I
looked into his eyes, which were far larger than mine but
shallower, and yellowed, the irises backed and packed with
tarnished tinfoil seen through the lenses   of old scratched
isinglass. They shifted a little, but not to return my stare. —It
was more like the tipping of an object toward the light. I admired
his sullen face, the mechanism of his jaw, and then I saw that
from his lower lip —if you could call it a lip— grim, wet, and
weaponlike, hung five old pieces of fish-line, or four and a wire
leader with the swivel still attached, with all five big hooks
grown firmly in his mouth. A green line, frayed at the end where
He broke it, two heavier lines, and a fine black thread   still*

crimped from the strain and snap when it broke, and he got away. Like medals with their ribbons frayed and wavering, a five-haired beard of wisdom trailing from his aching jaw. I stared and stared, and victory filled up the little rented boat, from the pool of bilge where oil had spread a rainbow around the rusted engine to the bailer rusted orange, the sun-cracked thwarts, the oarlocks on their strings, the gunnels—until everything was rainbow, rainbow, rainbow!

And I let the fish go.

Used By Permission

That fish was a real veteran who was released to fight another day.

Let's see what other extra-curricular activities might be available to you at this stop. While I'm thinking about it: Don't forget to keep those academic grades up to ensure your eligibility to participate in any of these activities.

Another area that you might consider is music. Learning to play a musical instrument can bring a lifetime of fulfillment. A man once asked a famous maestro how to get to Carnegie Hall. His answer: "Practice ". When asked how much he practiced, he replied: "When I don't practice for 2 days, my audience notices it. When I don't practice for a single day, I notice it". Constant practice and dedication under the tutelage of good teachers will bring success.

As I think of it, some of my clients enjoyed playing in marching and concert bands, and a few ended up playing in famous symphony orchestras.

You perhaps don't realize it, but you come with a built-in musical instrument: Your voice! You will have many opportunities to exercise those vocal cords. Perhaps it will begin with songs tied to nursery rhymes (I always thought "Twinkle Twinkle Little Star" had a certain ring to it) or perhaps songs you learn in Sunday school or the great "Songs of Zion", hymns sung in church. School and church choirs will provide other opportunities. One of my clients, along with three of his friends, formed a Gospel quartet and enjoyed singing to church audiences in their local area. You might discover a system called "karaoke" which plays the music while you supply the singing voice. Always remember to sing "Happy Birthday" along with others to honor the celebrant, and don't forget to remove your hat and hold it over your heart as you join others in singing your national anthem.

Along the way, you will develop a taste for certain kinds of music. From opera (Remember; it's not over 'til the fat lady sings) to country bluegrass (one of my clients dearly loved a song entitled "Rocky Top") to everything in between, you will discover certain genres that will tickle your sensibilities and become your favorite. The variety is endless.

We've covered a lot at this stop, so it's time to get back on board our time train and continue our passage to the next stop, one that will become one of the most important on your timeline.

CHAPTER 6
THE TEENAGE YEARS

Ages 13-19

We were young and strong,
We were runnin' against the wind.

Song by Bob Seger

Perhaps you will be feeling a little smug about reaching this stopover now that you are a big teenager, but let me warn you: these seven years can be the most difficult and dangerous of all on your passage. At this stop, you will face a complex array of challenges that can impact your physical, emotional, and mental well-being. If you think the dangers we covered at previous stops were a little scary, you ain't seen nothing yet. Teenage "rebellion" will reap the whirlwind.

Based on the latest data, here are the top five dangers affecting teenagers in your time slot:

1. **Unintentional injuries (Better known as accidents)**
    This leading cause of death includes motor vehicle crashes, falls, and other injuries. Since your level of good judgment is under development, you will tend to underestimate dangerous situations and make critical errors, leading to crashes. One of my previous clients, in the twentieth century, recalled an incident from a book he wrote that proves that point:

    > *"An adjunct of teenage rebellion was 'drag racing,' pitting one car against another. One driver would issue a challenge to another, after which all interested parties would drive to a selected location to witness the duel. These contests usually took place at night on a stretch of straight highway.*

    > *The two cars would then line up abreast, with a designated "flagman" standing out front between the two cars. With engines revved to the maximum, the two drivers would wait for the flag (usually a white handkerchief) to drop. At the first downward movement of the flag, the drivers would release their clutches and go screaming off into the night in a cloud of burning rubber and smoke. A finish line was painted across the highway one quarter of a mile ahead. A "judge" was stationed at the line to determine the winner. Having the fastest car was*

considered an honor, and he who had it was considered the "king" in the community.

In the fall of 1956, the professed "king" was a young man who worked at a local gas station. He had a low-slung Mercury that had been modified for drag racing. No one had come close to beating him for some time. And then one night, another young man showed up with a brand new 1956 Chevrolet V-8, one of the "hottest" cars on the market, and issued a challenge. After closing the service station, the "king pulled his car out onto the highway in front. Apparently, it was decided not to go to a safer location. The brand-new Chevy owner pulled up alongside. The flag was dropped, and the race was on. They raced down the highway side by side, past the quarter-mile mark, with neither giving in to the other. As they rounded a slight curve at estimated speeds of over a hundred miles an hour, the Chevy met an oncoming car in its lane, and with no place to go, hit it head-on. Both drivers died instantly, with the driver of the Chevy being decapitated in the process. People came from all over to view the wreckage, and it was agreed that the results of such an impact had never been seen before".

That story always gives me the shivers, but let it be the first lesson you learn when it comes to automobiles.

Statistics show that 38,000 people die in automobile accidents every year in the United States. Promise me that you will not be one of those at this stop. OK, we covered other types of accidents at previous stops, so let's move on to other dangers you are likely to face.

2. **Mental Health Issues**
    Mental health challenges, including depression and anxiety, are increasingly prevalent among my clients at this stop. The demons of loneliness, depression, family problems, being bullied, and substance abuse can contribute to suicidal thoughts. Each day in this nation, there are more than 3700 attempted suicides by young people between grades 9-12, many of them successful.

    Hopefully, you will find support at home, at your church, or at school should you ever entertain such thoughts.

3. **Risky behavior and substance abuse**
    "Hey! Watch this!" Those words are sometimes the preamble to a catastrophe involving injury and death. Never be a "show-off "or accept a "dare" that could cause you harm.

    What else is in this Pandora's Box of risky behaviors? Oh yes, I see things like unprotected sexual activity, tobacco smoking, including "vaping," alcohol use, dangerous driving, and other illegal activities like trespassing or vandalism. All these behaviors can lead to serious health and legal consequences. From such turn away.

4. **Social media and online exploitation**
    Excessive use of social media is increasingly being linked to mental issues such as depression and anxiety among teens. These platforms can expose you to cyberbullying, exploitation, and harmful content, influencing real-world behavior, which can lead to arrests for such things as sexual exploitation and terrorism. Hopefully, the authority figures in your life will help you strike a happy balance in the use of social media: at least until you are older and can understand the dangers.

5. **Bullying and peer pressure**
    I mentioned these to you previously, but I wanted to reiterate the dangers of these two significant issues for teenagers. Bullying can be in-person or online, physical or mental. It can lead to increased isolation, irritability, and difficulty sleeping. Peer pressure, manifested by the desire to be accepted, can also lead to underage drinking, drug abuse, suicidal thoughts, and other risky behaviors.

Whew! I'm ready for a break after all that. What's that you say? You don't want to stop at this station? Sorry, but it's a necessary rite of passage to get you ready for the next stop.

But don't despair. There are tons of good things that can come your way at this station. Let's consider the top five.

1. **Gaining Independence**
    Getting your driver's license and having your own car will be an exciting time. One of my clients told me how she got her first car. It seems that her grandfather wrote her a letter which went something like this, as I recall:

"Dear Granddaughter Sarah:

Believe it or not, I was in your very position at one time. I wanted a car in the worst way, not for transportation, I suppose, but for the freedom it offered. It was a very difficult time in my life, and I was embarrassed that I was not older and more independent than I was. The possibility of having my own car seemed like a distant dream.

Sensing my frustration, my father came up with an offer for me to consider:

If I worked during summer vacations from school, saved my money, did well in my school work, and helped out around the house, he would match what I saved, and I would have a car for my senior year in high school.

At the end of my junior year, I had saved $200 (Remember, this was in the 1950s). My father matched that, and we bought a 1940 Ford. I say we, because it had to be titled in his name. Plus, his insurance cost went up sharply with a teenage driver listed on his policy. He told me not to try to "straighten out any curves" with it, and if he ever heard of me driving recklessly, the car would be sold. I was super-excited now that I had "my" car. I now had the freedom and independence I longed for, but I was brought back down to earth by the fact that I had to continue to work to buy my own gasoline, plus run errands when asked.

What this is all coming to is this: I want to give you some hope in having your own car by making you a similar offer to what my father offered me. If you are willing to work full-time these next two summers and save your money, I will match what you save. Your parents can then help you come up with a car for your senior year.

Hang on a second while I check your file. Yes, you will have two grandfathers in this time frame. Perhaps one or the other will make you a similar offer. But let's move on to some other positive things that can happen at this stop.

2. **Personal growth and building long-lasting friendships:**
You begin to discover who you are, what you value, and what kind of a life you want to build at future stops on your passage. Plus, you will have the opportunity to build lasting friendships that will last throughout your journey.

3. **Developing a passion:**
You might discover a talent or hobby that you truly love- one that can stand the test of time and help make you feel alive throughout your passage.

4. **First love or "crush":**
Remember the other species of humanoids that you paid little attention to back on previous stops? Because of the explosion of hormones coursing through your body, your attention has been redirected to establishing a relationship with the female in your midst. While most of these passing relationships will only be considered "puppy love," it is possible to establish a deep relationship that can turn out to be your "soul mate" even at this early age.

5. **Mental and emotional growth:**
At this stop, you will learn to better handle emotions, challenges, and relationships, getting ready for that stop ahead called "Adulthood."

There are many other positive things that you will experience during this phase of your passage, but my time is drawing to a close. I have given you what I think is important when you live out these teen years. Follow your moral code, develop a spiritual relationship with your Creator, guard your heart, and you will do well at this station. Let's board the time train and see what lies ahead on your passage.

CHAPTER 7
ADULTHOOD

Ages 20-30

*"What lies behind us and what lies before us
are tiny matters compared to what lies within us".*

Ralph Waldo Emerson

That was a short ride, but here we are in the decade of the twenties, where a lot of amazing things can happen. This stop will likely set the tone for the remainder of your passage. It's often referred to as the "car, career, marriage, and house" decade. One thing is certain: you will go through a ton of changes and challenges, emotionally, socially, financially, and physically.

Back in your teen years, you probably wanted to be like everyone else in your peer group. Now, you will do an about-face with a desire to establish your own personal identity, completely different perhaps from your fellow travelers. You will begin to ask questions such as "Who am I?" "What am I going to do with my life?" It is here that you will possibly discover that purpose in life that we talked about earlier. Don't succumb to pressure to figure everything out at once. Luckily, time is on your side at this station. You will make mistakes, but that is part of the process. The future is wide open. You can change directions, reinvent yourself, and chase the American dream. Balancing passion vs practicality is the key.

Following my pattern, let's break down some of the common problems you might face:

1. **Choosing a Career**

    Finding stable or meaningful work can be a struggle. Don't yield to pressure to succeed early or keep up with your peers. Perhaps, like many, you will not have a clear idea of what you want to do. That is not unusual. Time and opportunity will guide you to your life's work. In the meantime, you might want to explore and /or experience the many employment options available, many of which will require additional education or technical training. One of my previous clients related this story about searching for a career:

    "My mother wanted me to be a doctor, so I enrolled in the Pre-Med program at the local university. After a couple of terms, the curriculum began to get serious about this career choice. And then I woke up one night with this pregnant thought: What if my passion becomes surgery? With my last name being "Butcher", I could just hear the hospital intercom calling out: 'Doctor Butcher! Report To Surgery, Stat!' I abandoned the idea of being a doctor at that point."

At times, even names can be a detriment to choosing a career. I recall one of my clients who was an airline pilot. One day, he received a written essay in the cockpit from a ten-year-old traveler who had already chosen his career.

It read as follows:

WHY I WANT TO BE A PILOT

I want to be a pilot when I grow up because it's a fun job and easy to do. That's why there are so many pilots flying around today.

Pilots don't need much school; they just have to learn to read numbers so, they can read instruments. I guess they should be able to read road maps, so they can find their way if they get lost.

Pilots should be brave so they won't be scared if it's foggy and they can't see, or if a wing or motor falls off. They should stay calm. Pilots have to have good eyes to see through clouds, and they can't be afraid of lightning or thunder because they are closer to them than we are.

The salary pilots make is another thing I like. They make more money than they can spend. This is because most people think plane flying is dangerous, except pilots don't, because they know how easy it is.

There isn't much I don't like, except that girls like pilots and all the stewardesses want to marry pilots, so they always have to chase them away so they won't bother them. I hope I don't get airsick because I get carsick, and if I get airsick, I couldn't be a pilot, and then I would have to go to work.

Out of the mouth of babes...

2. Avoiding Financial Stress

Would you want to be financially free when you get to the 40s decade on your passage? Starting as soon as you have a steady cash flow, follow the advice of those who made it. Here are some financial principles you will need to follow:

    i.   Avoid car loans if possible
   ii.   Avoid bad credit card debt and student debt
  iii.   Build your credit score
  iv.   Learn to live on a budget
   v.   Develop a separate stream of income
  vi.   Read more and limit your time with TV and social media
 vii.   Invest at least 10% of your income. You won't miss it, and it will accumulate quickly.
viii.   Build a 3–6-month emergency fund

Following these principles will be challenging. It will involve sacrifice, delayed pleasures, and many "Ramen Noodle" meals. Many of my clients have fallen into the debt trap, which has limited their degree of financial freedom far into their passage. Earning money is good. Saving money is better. Staying out of debt is the key.

3. **Physical and Mental Challenges**

You will want to develop healthy habits at this stop. Just because you came out of high school in great physical shape doesn't mean that that will continue unless you adopt a physical training regimen suited to your personal goals. Workout facilities are everywhere, with everything you need to maintain fitness at reasonable membership costs.

While there are many high-energy activities to choose from, most health experts suggest running and walking as the best choice to last a lifetime. Don't be a target for body-shaming by becoming a "couch potato". On the other hand, going at it too hard can lead to burnout and a poor work/life balance.

All things in moderation. Remember: Your health is your greatest wealth.

Mental health challenges at this stop can entail periods of anxiety, depression, and identity crisis centered around what it means to be a man. In this time period, there seems to be some confusion about that. You might receive conflicting messages from society, media, and even your family to "man up" or suppress your emotions. Lack of emotional support or failure to seek therapy can add to the problems you might face. Don't become isolated or disconnected in your social life.

It's important to develop strong masculine role models in your relationships. One of my clients chose to enter military service for that very reason. He told me: "I went in as a boy, I came out as a man". Bible study and continued spiritual growth will also reveal answers to life's questions.

4. Relationships

We talked about developing good relationships earlier, but in this stage of your passage, they become all-important. Relationships in the work environment can spell the difference between an enjoyable, successful career and one that will have you looking elsewhere. Some say that finding your" niche" in the overall scheme of things is the key.

Personal relationships are constantly changing in this stage as well. As time moves on, people grow apart. Evolving friendships can be challenging as people move in and out of your life.

The final, and perhaps the greatest challenge, will be navigating the minefield of things that could happen in a search for your "significant other." Figuring out the dating game is not for the faint of heart. Finding another person with a similar mindset and set of goals is not easy. You could find yourself in and out of temporary relationships with successive breakups or a long-term relationship, thinking you've found your "soulmate." Interestingly, people find each other in various places, primarily at work, in school, or through arranged activities. However, people at this stop are increasingly turning to social media and the many websites devoted to bringing people together. Since many people are delaying marriage, we will follow suit and cover that at the next stop.

Time to reboard our time train and continue our passage.

CHAPTER 8
THE THIRTIES

30-40

"Midlife is when the universe grabs you by the
shoulders and tells you:
I'm not fooling around. Use the gifts you were given."

Brene Brown

By the time you reach this stop, your personal growth and societal expectations will result in a unique set of challenges.

By this time, society says that you should have things figured out: your career, income, investment, and your path forward. Let's look at some of the obstacles you will be facing:

1. **Career pressure**
   Competition among your peers has never been stronger than at this juncture. One of my clients referred to it as a "rat race". He made a joke out of it by

saying, "Even if you win the race, you are still a rat." The important thing here is to avoid burnout, self-doubt, and disillusionment as you try to distinguish yourself above the crowd. Avoid developing a fear of falling behind if you see others getting ahead. Hard work, coupled with superior job performance, perseverance, and loyalty to the cause, will help ensure your upward mobility.

2. **Finances**

The proliferation of debt at this stop can become overwhelming.

Managing student loans, car loans, mortgage loans, and credit card debt, plus having something left over to save and invest, will require a financial plan-something not all young men were taught how to do. Perhaps it's time to engage a financial advisor to obtain that debt-free goal we talked about earlier.

3. **Marriage**

Perhaps the most important choice you will make at this stop, or any other stop, is the choosing of a bride- a life partner to share your passage. Commitment to a long-term relationship is a serious matter, and it is important to get it right the first time. While divorce rates have been falling in this timeframe, with many couples choosing to cohabitate, still 40-50% of marriages end up "on the rocks" with major life consequences, including financial loss, division of assets, emotional upheaval, and custody battles where young children are involved. Loneliness can set in as your status has changed. Friend groups change and will have moved on, leaving you with little support.

Here are some questions for your potential partner that should be considered before making that all-important marriage choice:

What are your financial goals, and how can we try to reach them?

Do you want children, and what would we do if we struggle to get pregnant?

What's your communication style?

What's your biggest fear?

What does marriage mean to you?

How much alone time do you need?

What are your relationship deal-breakers?

How can I help you when you are stressed?

How do we deal with our in-laws?

What are your expectations of sex?

These are just a few of the topics that should be discussed in that all-important, serious discussion that should take place well before any commitment.

Remember, your choice of a bride will reflect your character. In other words, in an odd way, she is you.

Other factors that should be considered during this pre-nuptial period might include:

> *What kind of family does she come from- a nuclear family or a broken home?*
> *What is her relationship with her father? The answer will tell you a lot about how she views men and portend her future relationship with you.*
> *What are her religious beliefs, and how do they compare with yours?*
> *Where will you live?*
> *Does she embrace God's plan for the roles each must play in a Christian marriage?*

I cannot stress enough how important it is to have these discussions before commitment. It will pay dividends down the road. Sometimes, in the heat of romantic love, they can be put on the back shelf and forgotten until it is too late to salvage the union.

So, where are you going to find this person to share your passage? Several of my clients made the mistake of searching the bars and night spots looking for a beauty queen, a "trophy wife "to display to the world. These searches don't normally turn out well. As I mentioned earlier, statistics show that most people meet their future spouses where they work, go to church, or in their leisure activities. Increasingly, couples are meeting and matching up on social media.

One of my clients told me how he met his future wife:

"I went into this bank one day to open an account. The New Accounts desk was not manned, so I was taken to the Bank President's secretary, who opened my account and, as my future wife, has been managing it ever since."

Well, I've beaten you over the head with this issue long enough. I predict that you will make a wise choice and enjoy a long and happy relationship.

Now to reboard our time train and move on to our next stop.

CHAPTER 9
THE FORTIES

40-50

"With adulthood comes responsibility, and with responsibility comes the weight of invisible burdens."

Unknown

While I wish I could forecast an easy time for you at this stop, it will probably be one of the more challenging ones on your passage. One day, you will suddenly realize that you are not twenty-one anymore. Coming to terms with aging and mortality can be emotionally jarring. Let's look at some of the physical changes that take place here as you age:

Slower metabolism and weight gain will make it harder to maintain muscle mass and avoid fat accumulation.

Declining testosterone levels will affect your energy, mood, libido, and physical strength.

Chronic health issues such as high blood pressure, diabetes, and heart disease can come into play.

Visible signs of aging, such as hair loss and wrinkles, can have an effect on your self-esteem.

Now that I have your attention, I cannot overstress the importance of getting regular medical checkups, following an exercise program, and breaking any bad habits you might have picked up along the way. Poor diet, smoking, and excessive drinking can end your passage prematurely.

If you and your spouse decided to have children at a previous stop, you would now have the added responsibilities of parenting young children or teenagers- a challenge that can be emotionally and physically draining. By taking an active role as the father figure and spiritual leader, you will reduce the frequency of behavioral problems, delinquency in sons, and psychological problems in daughters, all the while facilitating their cognitive development. Good luck.

This is a critical juncture in many other ways as well:

You might experience a "mid-life crisis", a time when you begin to have questions about life's purpose, past choices, and unfulfilled dreams. These factors can put a strain on your marriage. Steady as she goes here.

You now have to balance the demands of maturity with the pressures of aging, responsibilities, personal fulfillment, and time management.

Added stress may affect your family here as well. You might find yourself part of the "sandwich generation," caught between caring for aging parents and raising younger children.

Financial decisions can weigh heavily as you struggle with mortgages, saving for retirement, and funding children's education. Maintaining job security and a steady income flow are critical at this juncture.

Diminished career growth, particularly in fast-changing tech industries, can leave you stuck in a mid-level position or replaced by younger, cheaper workers.

Good mental health is also important at this juncture. Maintaining friendships, avoiding social isolation, and trusting the Creator for guidance will get you through to the next stop.

Speaking of the next stop, let's not be late for the time train. You can digest all we have covered here as we wait to board.

CHAPTER 10
THE FIFTIES

50-60

"When you have more years behind you than ahead of you, you think about life differently."

Scott Chittenden

The fifties are a "red zone" for men. Survive this decade, and your life expectancy will skyrocket because you got through the "danger zone". You might notice that this stop is eerily similar to the last one-a continuation of the challenges you might have faced at the last stop, only with a twist. Now, you can begin to enjoy some of the benefits of meeting all previous challenges. Some of those benefits might include the following:

You will have developed a clearer sense of priorities and values. With greater confidence and self-knowledge, you will feel more self-assured and less concerned about what people think. Peer pressure be gone!

In the area of your career, you might reach a leadership position or, with successful planning, reach that goal of financial stability as you work toward the elimination of debt. Home ownership and financial security are the goals. It's even possible that you might pivot into a new career if you have reached a peak in your work, or pursue some passion just waiting on the back burner.

Here, your relationships can become stronger. Marriage, friendships, and family ties deepen and become more meaningful.

You will now enjoy freedom from early-life pressures. Any children you might have had are now grown and more independent, giving you more personal time. It's possible that you will have more time and money to travel, pursue hobbies, or just relax from all your past efforts. Laz-E-Boy anyone?

Finally, you will have reached emotional maturity. Emotional regulation and your perspective on life take a positive turn. You will become more resilient and less reactive to challenges you still have to face. Continuing that spiritual relationship with the Creator is a key.

I hate to leave this area of positivity, but I have to preview the challenges you will face at this stop as well.

First, you might experience a decline in your health with issues such as high blood pressure, diabetes, weight gain, joint pain, reduced energy, and hair loss. Risks of prostate and heart disease increase. Maintaining an exercise program and getting regular medical checkups has never been more important for continuing your passage.

That midlife crisis or regret can continue at this stop as well. You might feel that you are "past your prime". Age discrimination can come into play as younger employees enter the workplace. Finding a new job or advancing your career may prove difficult. Your struggles with unfulfilled goals and feeling stuck in your career can lead to impulsive decisions or emotional distress.

Marriages can come under pressure due to long-term issues, the empty-nest syndrome, or personal changes resulting in divorce. In fact, statistics show that couples increasingly elect to seek a divorce in their fifties. The dating scene after divorce is not a pretty one. Second marriages end in second divorces sixty percent of the time. Avoid this mess by holding on to your faith and by seeking Christian counseling. Some of my clients have had ceremonies where they repeat their marriage vows and happily continue their passages together.

Even though your children have "left the nest", you are still part of that "sandwich generation". Caring for them, as well as for aging parents, can become a financial burden.

I hate to end with a sad note, but death can result in the loss of friends or loved ones. This is a sobering part of this stop on your passage. One of my clients jokingly stated that he checked the obituaries in the morning paper every day to see if his name was listed.

I see that my time is up, so let's get back on board our time train to see what lies ahead.

Are you feeling, O.K.?

CHAPTER 11
THE SIXTIES

60-70

"Don't look back. Something might be gaining on you."

Satchel Paige

At this stop, you will experience a wide range of life changes-some rewarding and fulfilling, others more challenging. Let's take a look at both the good and bad things that might occur at this stop.

If you have reached your financial goals from decades of saving and planning, you are ready for the big payoff and a chance to retire. This is a time for determining the income sources necessary to sustain you in retirement. Some of these would include pensions, savings, social security payments, and others. It is very important at this point that you are out of debt and that your home mortgage is paid off. You don't want to carry any long-term debt into your golden years.

Many people retire or reduce work hours at this stop, allowing more time for hobbies, travel, or family. With additional time and resources, pursuing that long-held passion can now become a reality. Losing the pressures of work and related career stress is an added benefit.

You can almost become a new person with a stronger sense of self, renewed confidence, and wisdom gained from life experience. You can now focus on what really matters with no concern for what others think. You have an improved perspective on life with greater emotional resilience and the ability to handle setbacks better. Your focus now turns to gratitude, maintaining good health, and developing meaningful social connections.

Family relationships deepen as you may enjoy the deeply joyful experience of becoming a grandparent. Your adult children become closer companions and sources of pride.

You will recognize many of the challenges at this stop as they are a continuation of those experienced at the last stop, the first being health issues. You may develop an increased risk of chronic conditions such as arthritis, heart disease, or diabetes. You may also notice that recovery from illness or injury often takes longer. Decreased mobility, energy, and stamina may create physical limitations. Activities once enjoyed may become harder to do.

You may also experience the loss of loved ones. Friends, siblings, or even spouses may pass away, leading to grief and loneliness.

Adjustments may become necessary as you begin your retirement years. You might experience a loss of identity or purpose tied to your career work. If you want or still need to work, you will discover age discrimination working against you in seeking new employment. You may experience feelings of being overlooked or undervalued.

As social circles change, isolation can become a problem as children may move away and friends may become less accessible due to distance or health.

If your financial planning has been adequate, you can avoid the strain of rising healthcare costs, inflation, inadequate savings, or dealing with unexpected expenses.

In summary, this stop can become a time of renewal, reflection, and reinvention—but it also often comes with challenges that require adaptability. Those who maintain strong social connections, stay mentally and physically active, and embrace a sense of purpose tend to thrive during this decade.

Our time train is scheduled to depart momentarily. Let's get back aboard and see what the next stop holds for your passage.

CHAPTER 12
THE GOLDEN YEARS

Part 2
70-80

"Time keeps on slippin', slippin' into the future"

"Fly Like an Eagle" Steve Miller Band

I hate to sound like a broken record, but this stop, for the most part, is a continuation of those covered at the last stop. Here, you will continue to experience a mix of positive and negative developments depending on your health, lifestyle, and life circumstances. Let's look at a balanced breakdown:

- You are now free from career pressures and, if you have planned properly, are enjoying a steady financial stream from your pension, investments, and savings.
- You now have more time for hobbies, travel, or volunteering, more time for enjoying your

grandchildren, and more time to deepen relationships with loved ones.

- Because of your decades of experience, you will now have greater patience, emotional stability, and a sense of what really matters. You will begin to focus on your legacy, using your ability to mentor younger people and pass down knowledge and traditions.

- Several of my clients wrote memoirs to chronicle their passage. Others made financial endowments to various universities for annual scholarship awards to outstanding students.

- You will now have better self-acceptance, less concern about other people's opinions, and more comfort in your own identity. You no longer have to "prove yourself" in work or social circles. If you are a veteran, you might experience more social respect. Plus, being an elder may boost your status and influence. Don't forget to take advantage of those senior discounts! Without fear of judgment, you can now stop holding back on expressing your opinions or style choices. Dig out those bright Hawaiian shirts.

- You might discover unexpected physical resilience. Some men actually improve fitness if they start exercising later in life. Just don't try to overdo it, as I said before: You're not twenty-one anymore. Walking has been named the best overall exercise at this stage. Lifting a few hand weights to build bone and muscle mass can also be of some benefit.

- You may experience greater romantic freedom, finding new relationships or rekindling intimacy without the pressures of raising children or building a career.

We now have to look at the challenges you will face at this stop:

1. Even if you are still healthy, you may become less mobile, making socializing harder without extra effort. Joint issues, muscle loss, and balance problems can limit activity. The danger of falling can create serious physical injury with a slower recovery time. Invisible health problems such as kidney decline and hearing loss can creep in unnoticed. You might have to be fitted with a hearing aid. You will also be subject to a higher risk of chronic health conditions such as heart disease, diabetes, and arthritis. You may experience a loss of independence requiring help with daily activities or a move into an assisted living environment. You might become more dependent on medications and other medical procedures in treating these conditions.

2. You may be subject to cognitive decline with risks of memory loss, dementia, or reduced mental sharpness. Depression and anxiety can arise due to isolation, loss of independence, loss of peers, friends, and loved ones. Adult children may take on a "parenting" role as you

confront fears of being a burden or worries about future care needs.

3. At times, you might feel overwhelmed, excluded, or dependent on others for help with new technology. Pressure can come from coping with family conflicts or living up to expectations.

Well, enough of that. As you can see, this stop will bring increasing challenges that must be met if you are to continue your passage. Speaking of that, I hear the time-train sounding the "all aboard." Let's see what lies ahead at the next stop.

CHAPTER 13
THE GOLDEN YEARS

Part 3

80-90

"You know you are getting old when the candles cost more than the cake."

Bob Hope

Following my pattern, we will first look at the good things that can occur at this stop:

1. While wisdom does not necessarily increase with age, (what's that old saying that there is no fool like an old fool?), You may gain a deep sense of perspective and clarity about what truly matters in life. One area to give some thought to is the long-time holding of anger or grudges toward something or someone. Researchers have shown that this tendency actually harms the

grudge-holder rather than the targeted recipient. One of my clients related an incident in his own life that helped him release that emotion:

Yes, here it is

THE LETTER

He was writing a letter as I came into the cockpit during a weather delay. Being nosy, I asked what he was up to. "Writing a letter to my father", he replied. I said, "Wow, you must be very close". "No, actually, I have hated my father all of my life."

"Then why the letter?" I asked. "Well, you see, this letter is to him, but it's actually for me. By telling him that I forgive him and that I love him, I can finally rid myself of the bitter root I've carried all these years."

It still seemed strange to me, but the more I thought about it, I realized that I, too, must write the same letter to my father who had abused me physically and mentally as I grew up.

The unburdening was instantaneous as the letter went into the mail, and I was allowed to go free. My father never mentioned the letter until the last time I saw him alive. He looked at me through tearful eyes and said, "Son, I'm holding on to that letter."

As you read this, perhaps you are one who needs to write that letter. If so, do it now. Only then will you and the addressee be able to go free.

Good advice, I must say.

1. This can also be a time of reflection and reminiscence.

My clients have left me a whole folder containing memories of their passages. Let's see. Here it is. I think you will enjoy some of these:

Simple rules for living were given to me by my grandmother

   i.   When it's daylight, get up.
  ii.   When it's dark, go to bed.
 iii.   If it starts to rain, come in the house.
 iv.   If it's cold, build a fire.
  v.   If it's Sunday, go to church.

You get the idea....

Oh, that we could live that simply in this chaotic world.

MOONSHINE

(NOT TO BE CONFUSED WITH "MOONLIGHT")

Jesse, is he okay" the old farmer asked as he glanced at the figure sitting in the car. "Yes, he's good," my father replied. The person in the car was General Mark Clark, hero of WWII and Commandant of the Citadel in Charleston, SC. The year was 1952, and the General had come to Tennessee to visit friends, do some fishing, and most of all, to get a taste of that Tennessee corn whiskey he had heard so much about.

My father, Conservation Officer for Union County, was assigned as his guide. Having roamed the county for years, he knew nearly every resident and the location of every illegal moonshine still. By not reporting those locations to the "revenuers," he was on good terms with the operators.

The old man stepped off the porch and disappeared around back, returning shortly with a half-gallon Mason jar filled with a slightly amber-tinged liquid. Putting it into a brown paper sack, he handed it to my father. "No charge, Jesse. Hope your guest likes the taste. It's the best run I ever made."

A few weeks later, my father received a letter from General Clark thanking him for his services. A PS at the bottom said: "I sure would like to get my hands on more of that fine Tennessee moonshine."

On that day, making moonshine was a common activity and a major source of income for many families. Cars were "souped up" to outrun the police on trips to the markets down south. A movie entitled "Thunder Road," starring the actor Robert Mitchum, was filmed to tell the story.

Today, anything labeled "Moonshine" is produced legally, and the few remaining stills are found only in museums.

Now you know why "all the folks on Rocky Top get their corn from a jar."

CAKE WALKS AND PIE SUPPERS

Fundraising has always been an important segment of our society. Organizations such as schools, churches, fire departments, etc., are constantly in search of revenue to fund extra benefits for their patrons.

While all but forgotten, cake walks and pie suppers were the primary means of raising money in many rural communities in times past.

Women and girls would bake the pies and cakes, put them into boxes tied with ribbons and other decorations, and bring them to the local school or church.

For the cake walk, chairs would be arranged in a circle with numbered squares placed in each seat. After purchasing a numbered ticket, participants would march around the chairs while music played. When the music stopped, each person would stand next to the closest chair, and a number would be drawn and called out. If your chair had that number, you received a cake.

The pie supper was more of a raffle and very much a courtship affair. Whoever won the pie got to share the pie with the girl who baked it. While the pie baker was to remain a secret, the word spread quickly as to whose pie was whose.

Growing up, I remember one event where a few pies went for huge amounts as the young men tried to outbid each other to be with their favorite girl.

Today, these events have been replaced by car washes, sales of cookies, candy, and fruit, and even GoFundMe sites on the internet- very efficient but never as much fun as a cake walk or a pie supper. God bless you.

HITCHHIKING

Never pick up a hitchhiker is a good rule to follow in this day and age. But it was not always so. In the innocent age that I grew up in, hitchhiking was a primary means of transportation for young men trying to get from point A to point B in the most economical way possible. With no car and very little money, there was no other way. And, there was an element of trust that existed between the vehicle owner and the prospective hitchhiker that neither would do the other any harm. It was not unusual to see people hitchhiking across the country, or to attend college, or to see that special girlfriend on the weekends. Living in a rural area, I remember hitchhiking to the local swimming pool. I would stand on the side of the highway with a rolled-up towel, hold out my hand with an extended thumb, and look expectantly at the approaching car. There were very few times when I wasn't picked up almost immediately, usually by a perfect stranger.

With the dawn of the high-speed interstate highway system and the moral decline of our nation, "thumbing a ride" has become a dangerous proposition. But it was not always so.

MISTLETOE

The giant pecan tree outside our house was known for two things: a perfect limb for hanging a swing and a large crop of mistletoe growing in its high branches. This parasitic plant was believed to have magical powers from ancient times and came to be a part of the Christmas decorating tradition. A sprig or ball of mistletoe hung above an interior doorway created a spot where any female standing under the mistletoe was subject to receiving a kiss. If she refused, it would result in bad luck for the coming year.

To harvest our mistletoe, my dad would load his 12-gauge shotgun and fire up into the branches, producing a rain of mistletoe which littered the ground. Added to a few branches of holly and pine, we had all our greenery for decorating the house.

RATIONING

Suppose you were told that you could only have 3 gallons of gasoline each week, or that your access to meat, butter, cheese, and even clothing, among other items, was extremely limited and based on the number of stamps you had in a ration book issued by the government.

That was actually the situation in this country from 1942 to 1946, where every American was issued a ration book. This gave everyone an equal shot at items limited by the need to feed and equip our armed forces during WWII.

I remember my mother sending me to the grocery store to see if meat or butter was available that day. We also had "meatless Tuesdays" and learned to use substitutes such as oleo margarine in place of butter. I also remember scrap metal drives and women folding gauze bandages for the Red Cross at the local church.

Those war years were years of extreme sacrifice. I wonder how today's generation would react under similar conditions?

God bless you.

S & H Green Stamps

From the 1930s to the 1980s, merchants developed reward programs to encourage customers to buy their products. (Perhaps it started with boxes of Cracker Jacks that came with an enclosed "toy".)

The largest of these reward programs was the introduction of S&H green stamps in the late 1950s. For each dollar spent, the merchant would issue a stamp, which was to be pasted into a booklet. Once booklets were full, they could be redeemed for various types of products at the local S&H Redemption Center. A catalog was provided, detailing the number of booklets required for each product.

I remember my mother being an enthusiastic participant in this program, making several trips to the redemption center with a paper sack full of booklets and furnishing our home with all kinds of "accessories."

There were many competing stamp programs out there, but S&H was the largest, often bragging that their merchants issued more stamps than the US Post Office.

Today, these programs have given way to instant "rewards" cards. While the customer does save at the cash register, it could never be as much fun as licking stamps, pasting them in a booklet, browsing through the catalog, and anticipating your trip to the redemption center.

Another of life's experiences has gone with the wind.

THE DRIVE-IN

Hard to believe, but it's true. There was a time long ago when there was no such thing as "social media": no My Space, no Facebook, no Twitter, no texting, no Smartphones. It was a kinder, gentler time when people actually interacted face-to-face using verbal conversation.

Except for social interaction at school or church (or sharing the family telephone that sat on a table in the hall), there was only one place to be: the local drive-in restaurant. It had names like Tastee Freeze, Blue Circle, Mel's, Krystal, Glyco's, etc., but whatever the name, they had this in common: they all served hamburgers, French fries, Coca-Cola, and ice cream-AND it was the only place to see and be seen by your peers.

The usual routine was to circle the drive-in to see which of your friends were there and to show off your car if you had just washed and waxed it. Then, if you had money, you could pull into an empty stall, join the other cars, and place an order. Soon, you and your friends started going from car to car, catching up on the gossip of the day and finding out who was going with whom.

I tried to capture that excitement recently and pulled into a Sonic Drive-In with my best girl. We ordered the food, but it just didn't taste the same. Plus, there were no 80-year-old teenagers there to share the news of the day.

God bless you.

FIREFLIES

It was that magical time on summer nights, after supper and before being called in to get ready for bed. While the old folks sat on the porch, their work done for the day, we kids would be out in the yard playing games like Red Rover or Hide-and-Seek (Whoopee- Hide we called it) or running foot races.

And then suddenly there would appear tiny flashes of light all around us. The lightning bugs had come out to put on their nightly show. We would catch some of them in our hands to examine more closely. Collecting several into a glass jar was also a common practice. Oak Ridge National Laboratory was actually paying kids to collect them for research.

Today, kids don't play outside as much at twilight. And too, the lightning bug is seen in fewer numbers due to pollution and development. Only in the Smoky Mountain National Park can one still witness the synchronized firefly shows of yesteryear.

May the fireflies come to your yard this summer.

SPRING GREENS

"I give every green plant for food, and it was so."

Genesis 1:30

When pioneer families emerged from their long winter habitations, the search began for fresh greens to add to their diet. That search was passed down to my grandmother and father, who knew what to look for and where to find it.

The first of these wild greens was watercress, which grew lush along the small streams in the early spring. I remember my father wading into the creek and harvesting a dishpan full. After my mother "stemmed" the leaves, they were "killed" with hot bacon grease and vinegar- a real delicacy. The famous New York restaurant Delmonico's actually had a watercress sandwich on its menu for its discerning clientele.

The second green variety ardently sought after was poke sallet (salad), derived from the poke weed- my grandmother's favorite. The shoots were cut as soon as they appeared above ground and cooked like asparagus. Interestingly, this plant was poisonous until cooked.

The third green variety was the Dry Land "Crease" (Cress), which my father dearly loved. He would scout the woods for this delicacy in early spring and never failed to come home with a sack full.

Finally, we come to the Ramp, a variety of wild onion that emitted a very pungent odor when cooked and ostracized all partakers from polite society when eaten. I remember going to The Ramp Festival is held annually in Cosby, TN. Tennessee Ernie Ford was the headline entertainer that year. You could smell the ramps cooking long before you got there. I just couldn't bring myself to indulge.

Today, the knowledge of wild greens available in nature has virtually disappeared. Now, every The grocery store has a wide variety of fresh greens, all boxed and ready to go.

But it was not always so.

BLUE JEANS THEN AND NOW

Yesterday being National Denim Day, I was wondering what is going on with America's iconic piece of leisure wear- the long-wearing denim blue jean? I understand that fashions change, but the transformation of this piece of clothing has gone from the sublime to the ridiculous. The department store Nordstrom has just introduced a pair of jeans smeared with fake mud to make it look like you are a "working man". The price for these "work" jeans is a staggering $425.00 dollars.

Back in the day, a pair of "new" jeans was a status symbol of sorts- something no young man would be caught dead wearing today. They have gone from new to faded to stressed to distressed, with rips and tears, and now to the addition of synthetic "mud." Levi Strauss must be turning over in his grave.

But I plan to have a pair of these jeans at a much lower cost. I'll just ante up $20 for a new pair, carefully crawl over some barbed wire, and through the nearest mud hole. Let dry and "Presto!" I'm ready to show the world how fashionable an old, overweight working man can really be.

God bless you.

Putting Up Hay

How would you like to be hot, sweaty, and itching all over for the last week of May? Dumb question, you might say, but that was my basic condition back in the day. Unfortunately, the last day of school seemed to coincide exactly with the first cutting of hay in our community. While other classmates were off to the lake and the area swimming pools, your humble author was relegated to the hayfields of north Knox County, Tennessee.

My father was part of a co-op with farmers in the area who grew hay for their livestock. One farmer cut the hay; another raked it into windrows, and another brought his baler into the field to finish the job. The bales were then divided among the members.

The loading, hauling, and "putting up in the barn" part is where I came in, along with a few other unfortunates. We always hoped for "string-tied" bales, as these were much lighter than the "wire-tied" bales that could go upward of 70 or 80 pounds and required gloves to handle. The worst part of the job was lifting the bales up into the loft of the barn, where it was stacked (see "itching all over" mentioned above).

Today, modern machinery has made harvesting hay a nearly hands-off operation- a totally unrecognized gift to the young schoolboys of today. But I don't know, perhaps something is lost in the process.

A Springtime Reminder

With the blooming of the beautiful cherry trees this time of year, I'm reminded of a song that my mother sang to me. The author is unknown, but the words teach a valuable lesson.

Little Cherry Blossom

Little cherry blossom lived up in a tree.

And a very happy little thing was she.

Clad all through the winter in a dress of brown.

Warm she was, though living in a northern town.

On one sunny morning, thinking it was May,

"I'll not wear this old dress today," said Blossom.

Mister Breeze, when hearing, very softly said:

"Do be careful, Blossom, winter is not dead."

Blossom would not listen, for the day was bright,

And she wished to glisten in her robe of white.

So, she let the brown one drop and blow away,

Leaving her the white one, all so fine and gay.

By and by, the sunshine faded from her view.

How poor Blossom shivered as it grew colder.

Ah! For that warm wrapper lying on the ground.

Now Jack Frost will nip her; he is prowling round.

Ah! Poor Cherry Blossom, she is in foolish pride,

Changed her proper clothing, took a cold, and died.

All you little children, listen and take care,

Go not clad too lightly, and of Pride beware.

This song made a big impression on me as a child, and I still tend to overdress in cold weather.

GOODBYE TO HAPPY TRAILS

If you are under 50, you won't understand any of this, but there was bad news out of Branson, MO last week. The Roy Rogers Museum was closed down, and all memorabilia was sold at auction by Christie's of New York, bringing 2.9 million dollars. Gone are Trigger (stuffed), billed as the smartest horse in the movies; Bullet (stuffed), the Wonder Dog, plus a myriad of saddles, boots, shirts, and hats worn by Roy and his wife, Dale Evans, in the hundreds of movies and TV episodes they made together. Even "Nellybelle," the jeep fell under the auctioneer's gavel.

With the demise of the museum (for lack of interest, it was said), a part of my childhood goes with it- Saturday mornings at the local theater, when Roy and other "singing cowboys" raced across the silver screen fighting for truth, justice, and the American way, while all of us in the peanut The gallery cheered them on. They were our heroes, and, as a result, we developed a keen sense of right and wrong, good and evil, in the world around us.

Not so much for the younger generations of today. With violent video games, near-pornographic movies and social media being what they are, there is little to recommend the assimilation of a good value system. In fact, suicide is the second leading cause of death for children 10-14 years of age.

Perhaps someone will come to the rescue and introduce Roy Rogers and other western heroes to a whole new generation.

Happy Trails to you.

One of my pilot clients reminisced about simple rules to go by when flying, and left a poem to express the emotions he experienced during his time in flight:

RULES FOR FLYING

My old flight instructor, Elmer Wood, gave me the first rules of flying. He said:

Never fly at night, in the weather, when the wind is blowing, or if someone is shooting at you.

The rest of the time, do it VERY CAREFULLY!

I wish I had listened to him, because I had to do all of those things over the course of my career as a pilot.

But, on the other hand, think of all the moments of stark terror I would have missed.

HIGH FLIGHT

John Magee

"Oh, I have slipped the surly bonds of earth,

And danced the skies on laughter-silvered wings;

Sunward I've climbed and joined the tumbling mirth

of sun-split clouds —and done a hundred things

You have not dreamed of–wheeled and soared and

swung high in the sunlit silence.

Hovering there, I've chased the shouting wind along

and flung my eager craft through footless halls of air.

"Up, up the long delirious burning blue

I've topped the wind-swept heights with easy grace,

where never lark, or even eagle, flew;

and, while with silent, lifting mind I've trod

the high untrespassed sanctity of space,

put out my hand and touched the face of God."

MEMORIES, MEMORIES, MEMORIES

Being a grandfather or a great-grandfather can bring great joy and purpose. Sharing knowledge and stories like these can strengthen family bonds and provide a link to the past. As I said earlier, some of my clients have written their memoirs at this stage, providing a detailed story of their passage.

1. You can enjoy even more freedom from work pressures and responsibilities, meaning more time for hobbies, travel, or relaxation. You might consider divesting yourself of the big family home and scaling down to something smaller and easier to maintain. Buying into an independent living facility is another option.

2. By this time, most men know themselves well and feel less pressure to prove anything. Friendships and partnerships can become deeper with less conflict and more appreciation. Volunteering, mentoring, or joining groups can give a renewed sense of purpose.

As always, there is a flip side to every coin. Let's look at the challenging or difficult things that can happen at this stop:

While advancements in modern healthcare and treatments have allowed men to live healthier, longer lives than previous generations, there are still day-to-day issues that have to be confronted. Let's look at some of the more important issues:

i. **Physical decline** - your challenges here will involve reduced strength, slower recovery from injury and illness, and mobility issues. You might need a cane or a walker to help you get around and to help you overcome the fear of falling. Hearing loss is common, requiring the use of hearing aids and the adjustment problems they create. Your eyesight may start to dim, requiring cataract surgery and adjustment to eyeglasses.

ii. **Chronic Illness** - Conditions like heart disease, diabetes, arthritis, or cancer become more prevalent. Cognitive decline can produce memory problems or dementia that can affect independence and relationships. Frequent doctor visits, hospitalizations, or reliance on medicines can become overwhelming.

iii. **Loss of Independence** - You may find yourself beginning to rely on caregivers, needing help with daily activities, or a move into an assisted living or memory care unit after a professional evaluation.

iv. **Loneliness, Isolation, and Bereavement-** Friends, spouses, siblings, and good friends may pass away, leaving you to cope with their loss. Social circles can shrink, leaving you alone.

v. Other factors include fear of mortality as you become more aware of limited time, bringing on increased anxiety and depression. You may no longer be the provider or central family figure. Retirement savings may not stretch as long as expected, leading to stress.

Let me interject a thought here:

God, the Creator, wants you to be happy. Sorrow, depression, and isolation can lead to a premature death and the end of your passage. Self-pity is another destructive behavior related to selfishness. Don't become so absorbed with yourself that you ignore the situation of others. One of my English clients always said, "Keep a stiff upper lip" in the face of difficult circumstances, and always keep your social calendar full.

Let's now look at two daily scenarios that a man in his 80s might lead on the best of days and the not-so-best of days.

A Good Day in His 80s (Best-Case Scenario)

- **Morning:** Wakes up rested, makes breakfast with his spouse, or enjoys coffee while reading his daily devotional. Goes for a light walk or does gentle exercise.
- **Late Morning:** Calls or visits with family; maybe babysits a grandchild for a few hours. Feels proud being "the wise elder."
- **Afternoon:** Works on hobbies—gardening, woodworking, painting, or golfing with friends. Volunteers at a local club or community center.
- **Evening:** Shares dinner with loved ones, enjoys a TV show, book, or music. Reflects on the day with contentment.
- **Night:** Goes to bed with a sense of peace, purpose, and connection, thanking the Creator for all His blessings

A Difficult Day in His 80s (Challenging Scenario)

- Morning: Wakes up stiff or in pain, struggles with getting dressed. Needs medication reminders. Might feel frustrated about the loss of independence.
- Late Morning: Feels isolated—friends have passed, family is busy, and loneliness sets in. Memory lapses cause worry or embarrassment.
- Afternoon: Limited mobility keeps him mostly indoors. Doctor's appointments or health concerns dominate the day. Financial worries may linger.
- Evening: Eats alone or in silence, watches TV out of habit. Misses his spouse or old friends deeply. Reflects on life with sadness or fear of decline.
- Night: Has trouble sleeping due to pain, anxiety, or health issues. Worries about being a burden or about mortality.

In reality, most men in their 80s experience a mix of both scenarios—good days where they feel engaged and valued, and harder days where health or loneliness weighs heavily.

So how can men in their 80s create more good days?

1. **Physical Health** - Stay active to help maintain mobility, balance, and mood.

    Eat well: a balanced diet supports energy and prevents frailty.

    Medication management: Organize daily doses to avoid mix-ups.

    Regular Checkups: Preventive care can catch issues early and reduce emergencies.

2. **Mental and Emotional Well-being** - Keep the mind sharp by reading, puzzles, learning new skills, etc.

    Engage passions: music, art, gardening, or writing can bring joy and purpose.

    Mindfulness: meditation and prayer can reduce stress, while men's support groups can help process grief, anxiety, or depression.

3. **Social Connections:** Stay connected to family with regular calls, video chats, or visits to reduce loneliness.

Friendships matter: clubs, senior centers, or faith groups can provide companionship.

Mentoring younger generations: passing down wisdom gives a sense of legacy and usefulness.

Companionship from pets: Caring for a dog or cat can ease isolation.

4. **Daily Life and Independence:** Adapt the home with grab bars, good lighting, and mobility aids to prevent falls and give confidence.

Keep a routine: Structured days reduce boredom and help with memory.

Ask for help when needed: Accepting support with meals, transport, and cleaning can prevent being overwhelmed.

Focus on things that can still be enjoyed. Plan ahead by having finances, wills, and healthcare preferences in order to reduce stress.

Finally, boost positivity by reflecting on small joys and showing gratitude to the Creator each day.

Whew! That is a lot to remember, but all very important to continue your passage beyond this station. We have spent an inordinate, but necessary, amount of time here to prepare you for the last station and the end of your earthly passage.

Here comes our time train.

All aboard!

CHAPTER 14
THE GOLDEN YEARS

Part 4
90-100

"The end of a thing is better than the beginning".

Ecclesiastes 7:8

If you arrive at this station on your passage, you will have reached a milestone that many never reach. All the same joys and challenges continue here, but are more pronounced.

As a respected elder, you will be seen as a source of wisdom, history, and perspective to younger generations. Birthdays in the 90s are often major events filled with family appreciation and recognition.

You are now at peace with life, especially if surrounded by love and support.

With a slower pace of life and simplified priorities, you have time to rest, reflect, and enjoy simple pleasures.

On the other end of the spectrum, you may experience severe physical decline, including frailty, difficulty walking, dependence on wheelchairs, and a higher risk of falls. Chronic illnesses and fatigue are often more advanced. Cognitive decline also becomes more common, making daily life harder.

A loss of independence may require help with dressing, bathing, eating, or moving around. Hearing and vision loss make communication harder.

By the 90s, most peers, siblings, and often a spouse have passed away, shrinking your social circle and increasing your isolation without active family involvement.

End-of-life concerns, such as financial and care needs, may dominate your thinking, as will an increased awareness of mortality and becoming a burden.

EPILOGUE

To Canaan's Land I'm on my way.

Where the soul never dies.

My darkest night will turn to day

Where the soul never dies

Gospel song by Ricky Skaggs

POST-PASSAGE BRIEFING

You will notice that the time-train has come to a stop with no way forward. While there are a very few passages that will go beyond the century mark, there aren't enough to warrant the construction of another station. They all fall back to this one.

At this point, you will have come as far as you can go in human flesh. The moment you are conceived, you are destined for this end. Regardless of the circumstances, the Creator's perfect will determines the length of your passage.

So where would you go from here?

Just to the west of this station, there is a tunnel where all living flesh must enter. Initially, it will be very dark, but soon you will see a bright light ahead, which will guide your steps. As you continue toward that light, you will be translated beyond the curtain of time in a process called death. As I mentioned earlier, your human body will return to the dust of the earth, your spirit will break up, and your soul will be clothed with a spiritual body called a theophany. You will then be back in the stream of eternity - part of the ceaseless ages with all troubles and pain of human existence behind you.

When you leave the tunnel, you will come to a river called the Jordan. As the children of Israel crossed the natural Jordan to enter the Promised Land, so will you be transported across the spiritual Jordan to the spiritual land called Canaan. I'm told that in many cases, loved ones who have gone before will be there to meet you.

You will now be in a holding area. Since you were marked as one of His, you will wait there for the secret coming of the Lord, an event called the Rapture or the first resurrection. His chosen ones will awaken, take on glorified bodies, and rise to meet the Lord in the air, where they will be with Him forever.

Those souls that are left behind will sleep for another thousand years and then be awakened in the second resurrection to appear for judgment at God's great white throne.

It is now time for your preview to come to a close. We will now take a non-stop express trip on the time train back to your embarkation point. It is almost time for you to be born, and I have to meet another client for my next preview.

While all I have shown you will be erased from your prenatal brain, maintaining a close relationship with the Creator during your passage will produce benefits. He has promised that His Holy Spirit will guide you into all truth. Will you have troubles? Absolutely! But remember the words of the god-man Jesus Christ: "In this world you will have trouble, but take heart; I have overcome the world."

Good luck and Godspeed.

BIBLIOGRAPHY

Child Psychology & Development for Dummies
Laura L. Smith & Charles H. Elliot, PhDs
Wiley Publishing

Wikipedia Online Encyclopedia and ChatGPT

Google Search

The Message
1100 sermons by Reverend William Branham

The Holy Bible
NIV Translation

NOTE FROM THE AUTHOR

Let me say upfront that I am not a theologian or affiliated with any denomination or organization. All spiritual references used in this project are from my own understanding of biblical scripture as learned over my lifetime under the teaching of anointed men of God. In the event that your view of anything presented herein should differ, I can only say that I respect your opinion. God deals with us as individuals, and he has dealt wonderfully with me. God bless you.

OTHER WORKS BY
D. Allen Butcher

SIXTY YEARS IN THE TWENTIETH CENTURY

A Pilot's Memoir

ISBN: 1475084145

Create Space, North Charleston, SC